THIS **ELEPHANT & PIGGIE** BOOK
BELONGS TO:

_____

_____

_____

For Lowell, Lee
and Chelsea

Are You Ready to Play Outside?

By **Mo Willems**

WALKER BOOKS
AND SUBSIDIARIES
LONDON · BOSTON · SYDNEY · AUCKLAND

An **ELEPHANT & PIGGIE** Book

Piggie!

Gerald!

Are you ready
to play outside?

14

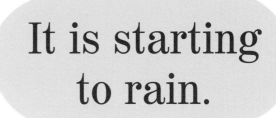

It is starting to rain.

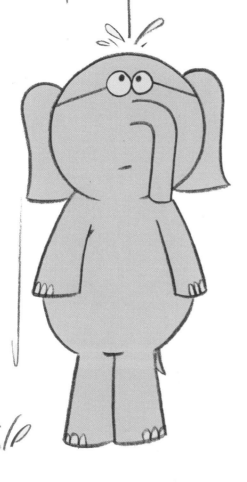

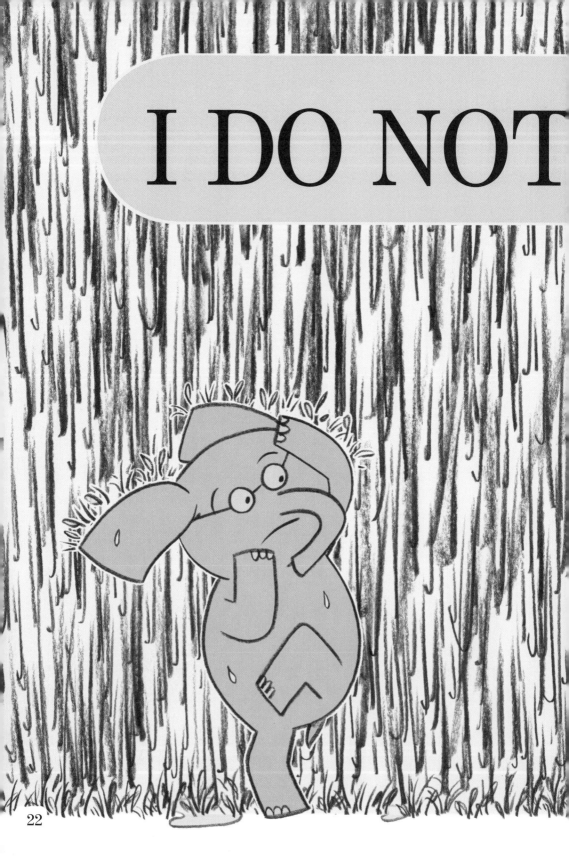

I DO NOT

HOW CAN ANYONE PLAY OUTSIDE WITH ALL THIS RAIN?!

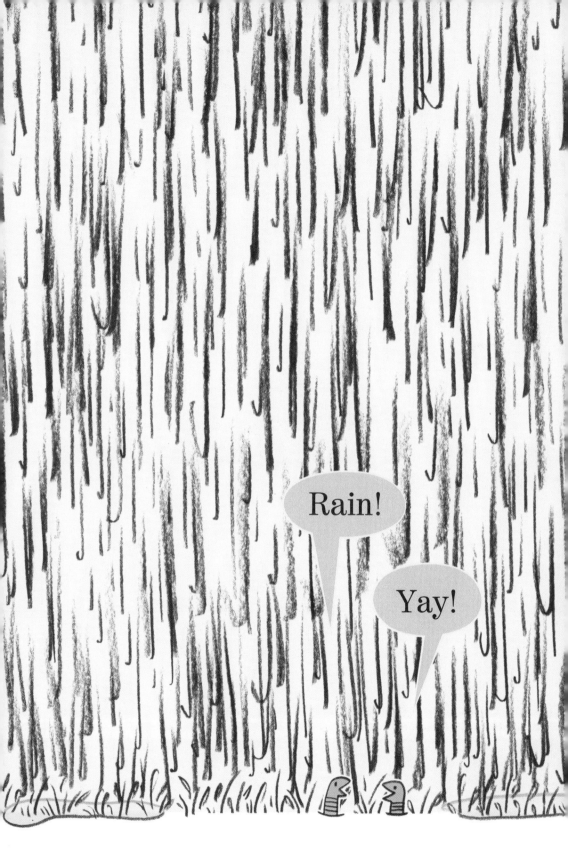

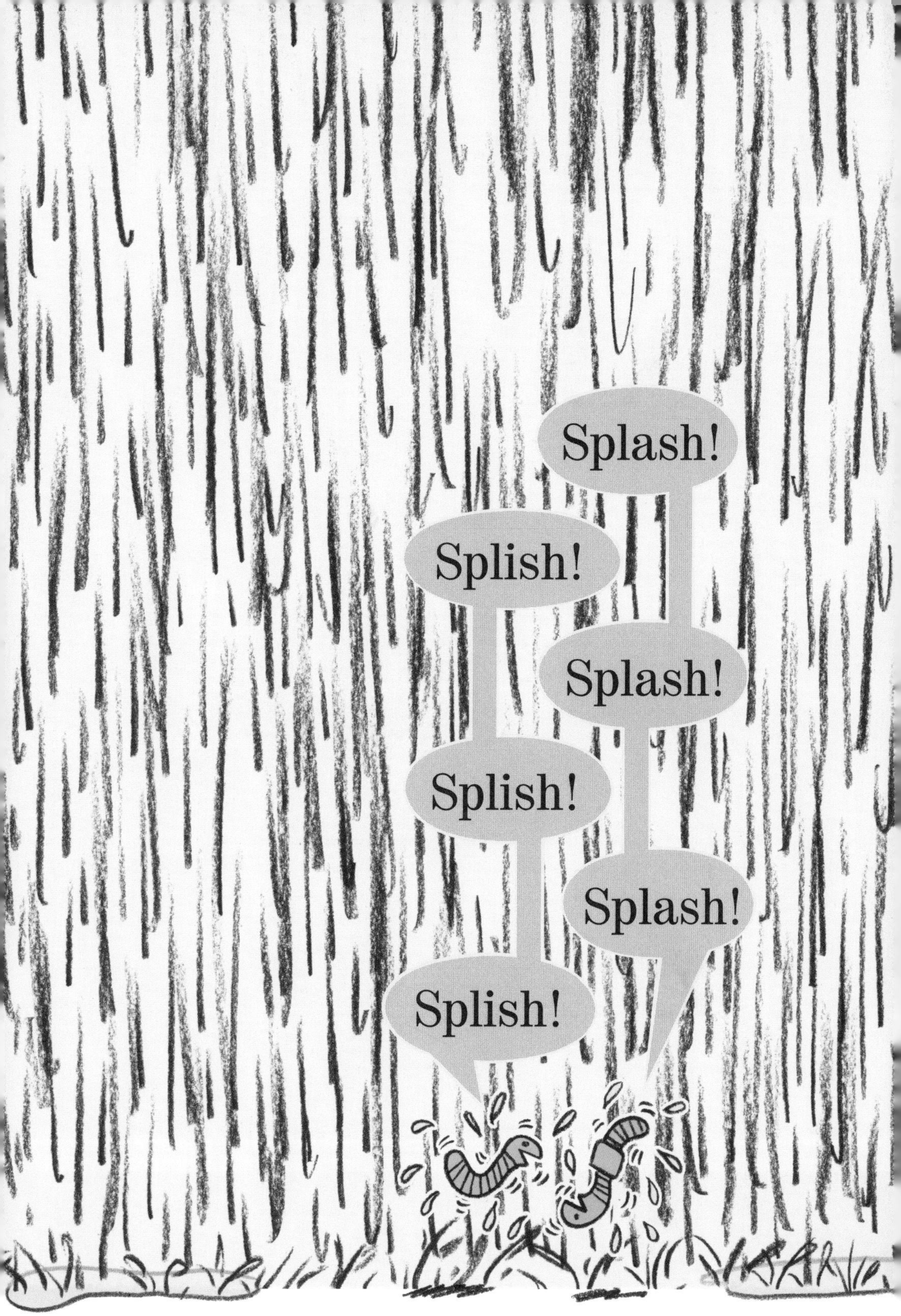
Splash!
Splish!
Splash!
Splish!
Splash!
Splish!

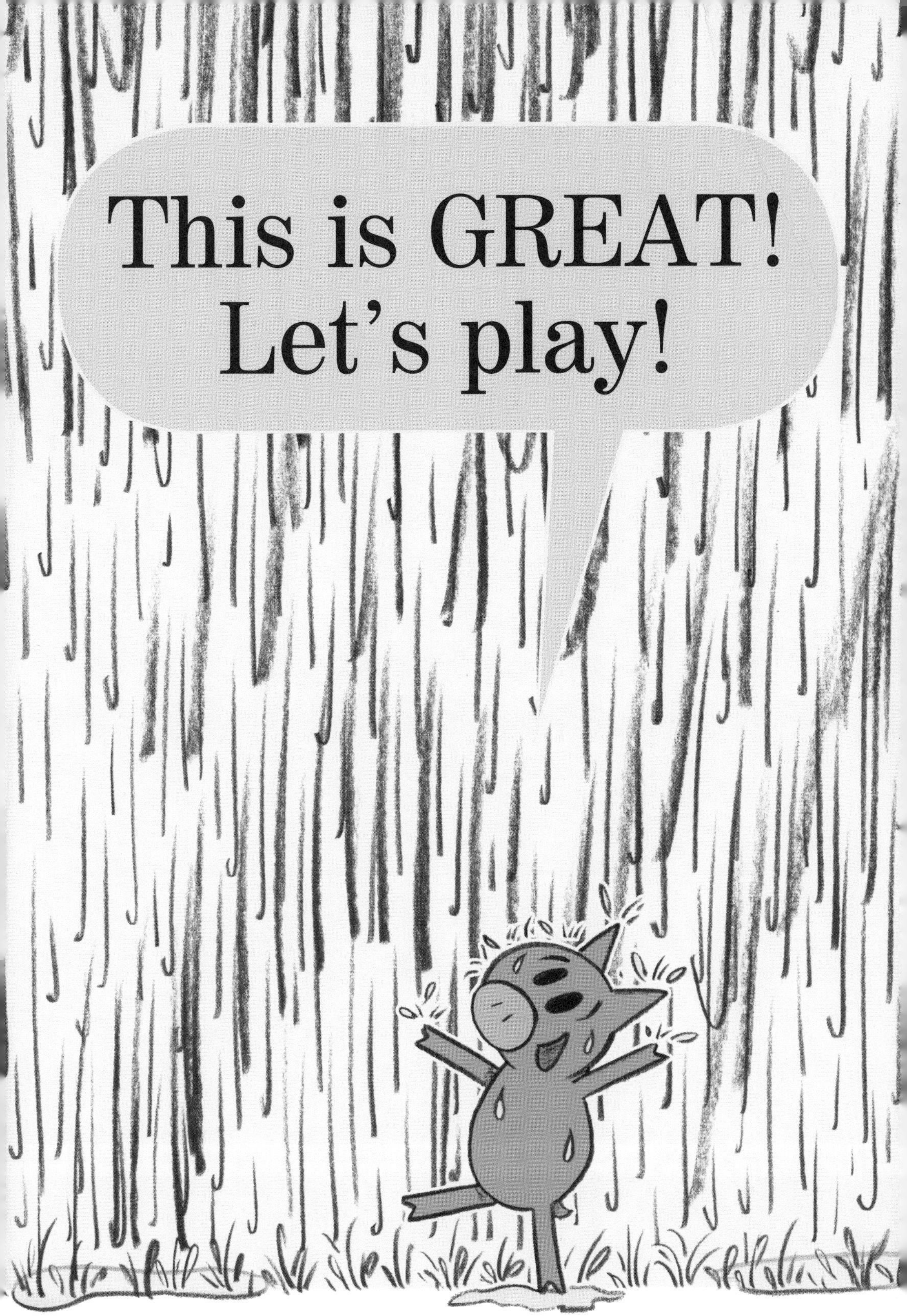
This is GREAT! Let's play!

49

Rats.

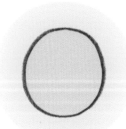

Now I like rain…

And now the rain has stopped!

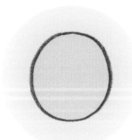

I am not a happy pig.

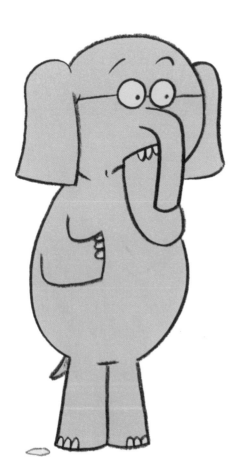

56

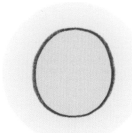

Do not worry, Piggie.
I have a plan.